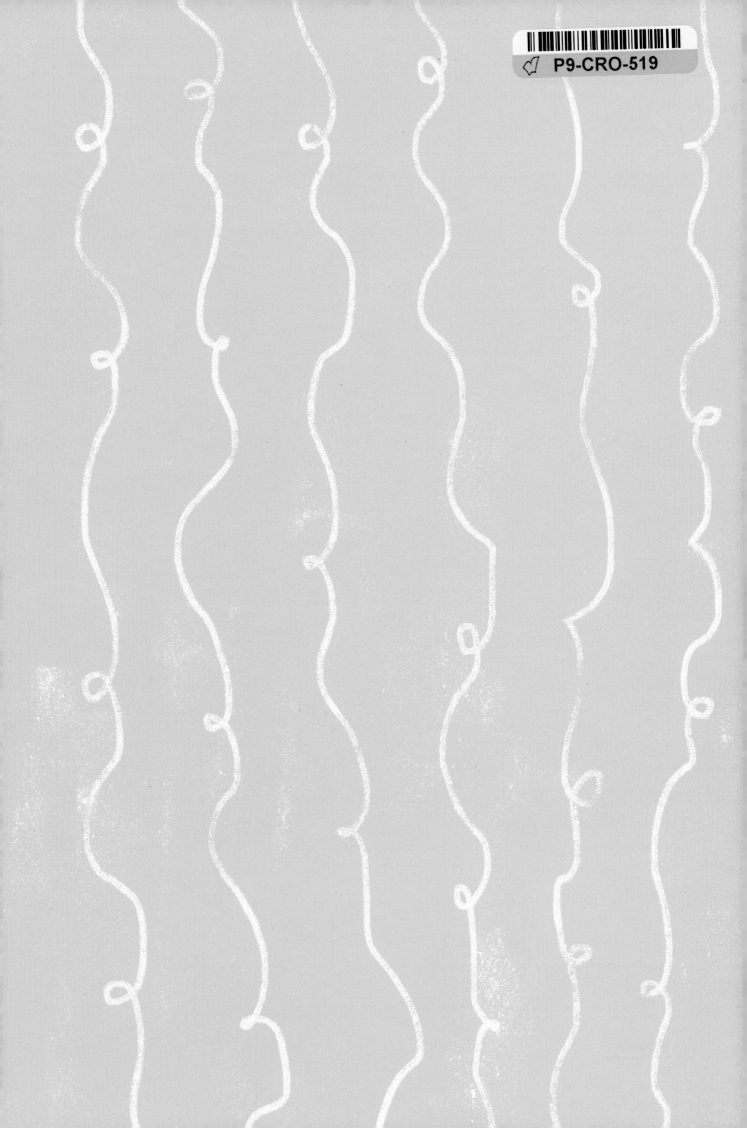

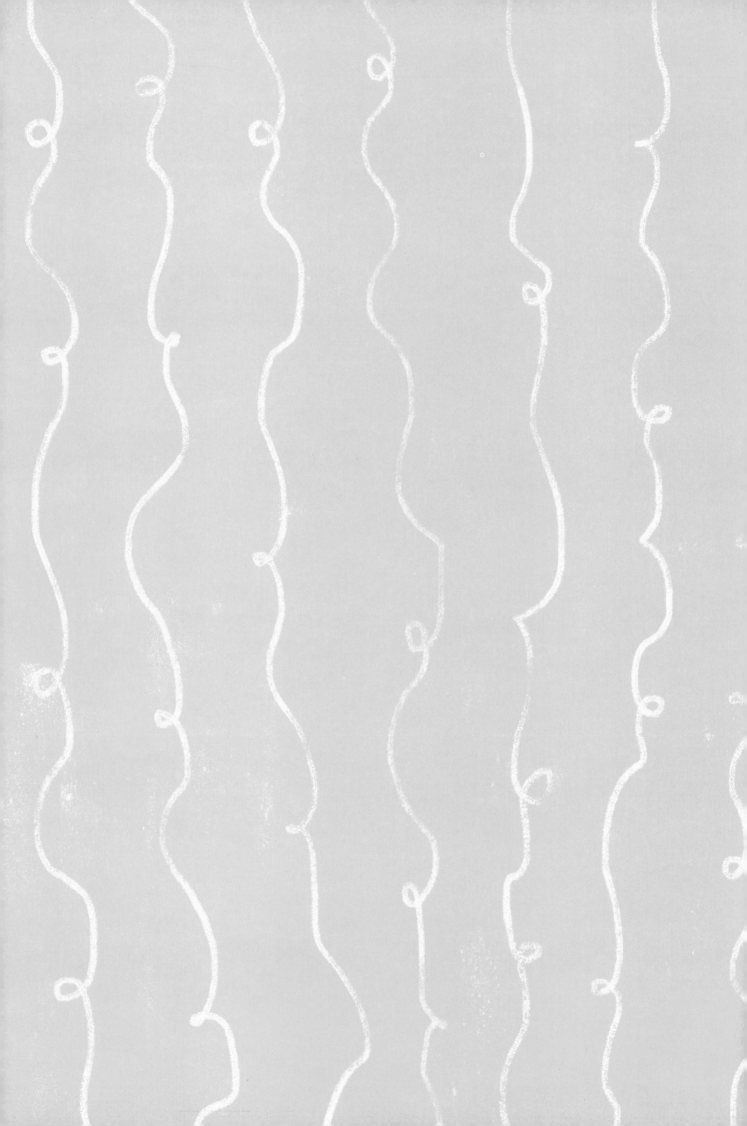

For Joy-Shanti, Indigo, and Serene.
−M.E.T

For Eva, and every free spirit
with a wild heart.
−A.C

www.enchantedlion.com

First published in 2019
by Enchanted Lion Books
67 West Street, 317A,
Brooklyn, NY 11222

Text Copyright © 2019 by Mariahadessa Serene Tallie
Illustrations Copyright © by Ashleigh Corrin Webb
Art Direction: Claudia Zoe Bedrick
Graphic Design: Ashleigh Corrin Webb
Layout and Production: Eugenia Mello

Printed in June by R.R. Donnelley Asia Printing Solutions

ISBN 978-1-59270-288-6
First Printing

Written by
MARIAHADESSA EKERE TALLIE

illustrated by
ASHLEIGH CORRIN

Layla's Happiness

ENCHANTED LION BOOKS
NEW YORK

My name is

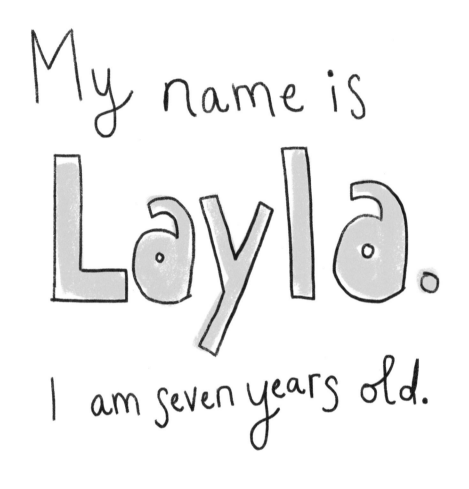

Layla.

I am seven years old.

Layla means "night beauty,"

and I love the night.

The dark
sky is
pretty.
It's the color
of dark,
purple plums.

And the full moon — well, it's my favorite.

It sits in the sky like a

wish flower's sister.

If I could reach the moon,

I'd **blow** on it and

wish to play the trumpet well,

without ever having to practice.

I think happiness is climbing a tree,

or

wearing

purple,

or eating
spaghetti
without a fork.

It's **my dad**
when he talks about
growing up in South Carolina,

and my
mom
when she
reads
me
poetry.

Happiness is planting a tomato seed and watching it grow in my favorite place—the community garden down the block.

In the garden,
I can dance
with a ladybug
on my finger,

see butterflies,

and chase my friend, Juan.

I can feed chickens
and give all the trees names.

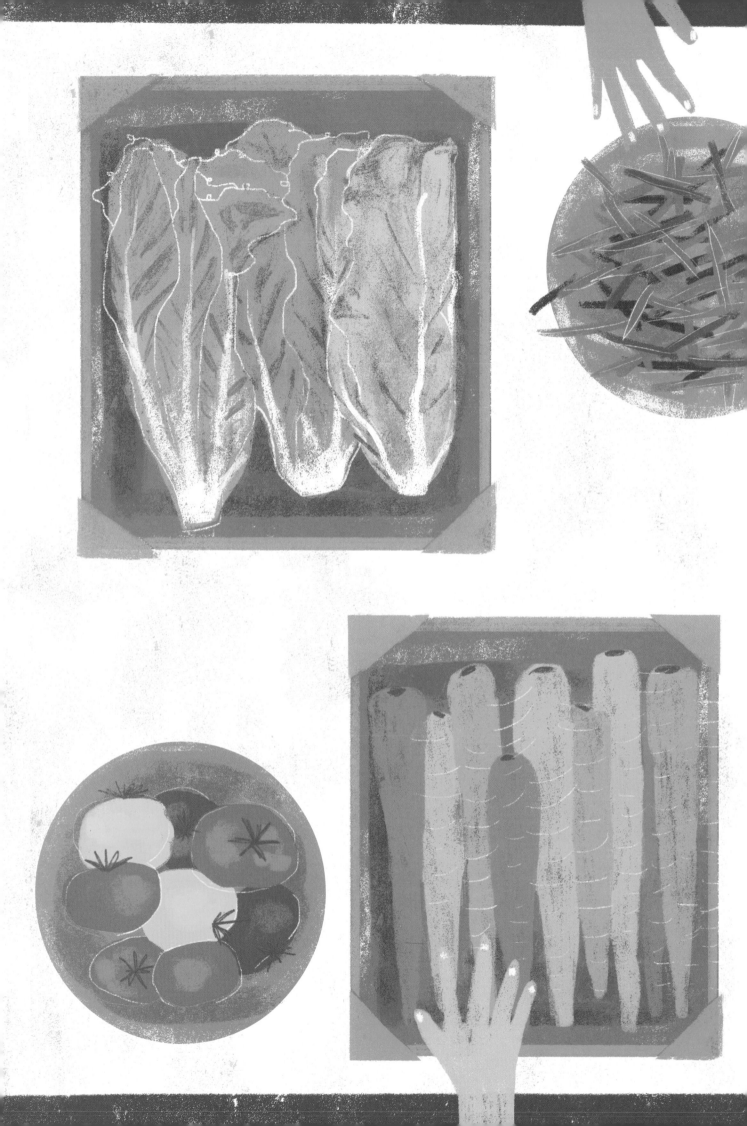

I can even pick vegetables
to sell at our farmer's market.

I think happiness is
hearing Juan's parents
laugh after they
dance salsa
under the magnolia tree.

And when the sea
reaches into her pocket

I think happiness is showing my mom the **outer space flowers** in my kaleidoscope.

That's what
I think.

Do YOU think so too?
What is happiness to you?